SHREK!

WILLIAM · STEIG

FARRAR · STRAUS · GIROUX · *New York*

To Emma, Jonathan, Alicia, Will, Kate, Jonas,
and Carol Regnier

Copyright © 1990 by William Steig
All rights reserved
Library of Congress catalog card number: 89-61252
Distributed in Canada by Douglas & McIntyre Ltd.
Printed in the United States of America
Designed by Atha Tehon
First edition, 1990
Sunburst edition, 1993
21 23 25 24 22 20

ISBN-13: 978-0-374-46623-7 (pbk.)
ISBN-10: 0-374-46623-8 (pbk.)

His mother was ugly and his father was ugly, but Shrek was uglier than the two of them put together. By the time he toddled, Shrek could spit flame a full ninety-nine yards and vent smoke from either ear. With just a look he cowed the reptiles in the swamp. Any snake dumb enough to bite him instantly got convulsions and died.

One day Shrek's parents hissed things over and decided it was about time their little darling was out in the world doing his share of damage. So they kicked him goodbye and Shrek left the black hole in which he'd been hatched.

Shrek went slogging along the road, giving off his awful fumes. It delighted him to see the flowers bend aside and the trees lean away to let him go by.

In a shady copse, he came across a witch. She was busy boiling bats in turpentine and turtle juice, and as she stirred, she crooned:

"This is the way I cook my bats,
    Stir my bats, taste my bats,
    Season my bats in the morning;
    Stew and brew and chew my bats,
    Diddle and fiddle and faddle my bats,
    Early in the morning."

"What a lovely stench!" Shrek cackled. The witch specialized in horrors, but one single look at Shrek made her woozy.

When she recovered her senses, Shrek said, "Tell my fortune, madam, and I'll let you have a few of my rare lice."

"Splendid!" crowed the witch. "Here's your fortune.

"Otchky-potchky, itchky-pitch,
Pay attention to this witch.
A donkey takes you to a knight—
Him you conquer in a fight.
Then you wed a princess who
Is even uglier than you.
Ha ha ha and cockadoodle,
The magic words are 'Apple Strudel.'"

"A princess!" Shrek cried. "I'm on my way!"

Soon he came upon a peasant singing and scything. "You there, varlet," said Shrek. "Why so blithe?"

The peasant mumbled this reply:

> "I'm happy scything in the rye,
> I never stop to wonder why.
> I'll hone and scythe until I die.
> But now I'm busy. So goodbye."

"Yokel," Shrek snapped. "What have you in that pouch of yours?"

"Just some cold pheasant."

"Pheasant, peasant? What a pleasant present!"

The last thing the peasant saw before he fainted was Shrek's glare warming up his dinner. Shrek ate and moved on.

Wherever Shrek went, every living creature fled. How it tickled
him to be so repulsive!

Fat raindrops began sizzling on Shrek's hot knob.

"Did you ever see somebody so disgusting?" said Lightning to Thunder.

"Never," Thunder growled. "Let's give him the works."

Lightning fired his fiercest bolt straight at Shrek's head. Shrek just gobbled it, belched some smoke, and grinned. Lightning, Thunder, and Rain departed.

In high spirits, Shrek stalked on. At the edge of a woods, he found this warning nailed to a tree:

> *Harken, stranger.*
> *Shun the danger!*
> *If you plan to stay the same,*
> *You'd best go back from whence you came.*

Shrek, of course, swaggered right past.

And sure enough, a little way into the woods, a whopper of a dragon barred his path. Shrek smiled and bowed. The dragon slammed him to the ground, but Shrek just lay there. He was amused.

The irascible dragon was preparing to separate Shrek from his noggin.
But Shrek got him between the eyes with a putrid blue flame.
The poor dragon thudded over, unconscious for the day.

An hour later, Shrek himself was unconscious. He had fallen asleep along the way. He dreamed he was in a field of flowers where children frolicked and birds warbled. Some of the children kept hugging and kissing him, and there was nothing he could do to make them stop.

He woke up in a daze, babbling like a baby: "It was only a bad dream...
a horrible dream!"

Shrek wandered on. He was wondering if he'd ever meet his princess, when he saw a donkey grazing. Was this the donkey the witch had foretold? Shrek hurried over and tried the magic words: "Apple Strudel!"

The donkey raised his sleepy eyes and brayed:

> "I gaze in the green
> As I graze in the green,
> Seeking out the clover.
> I laze and spend my days in the green,
> A chewing, chomping rover."

"You jabbering jackass!" Shrek screamed. "Aren't you supposed to take me somewhere?"

"I am. To the nutty knight. Who guards the entrance. To the crazy castle. Where the repulsive princess. Waits."

"Then take!" Shrek shrieked, and he hopped onto the donkey's back.

They soon came to a drawbridge where a suit of armor stood. Shrek knocked on the breastplate and demanded: "Who dwells inside this armor, and also in yonder castle?"

"In here a fearless knight, in there a well-born fright" was the answer.

"It's my princess!" said Shrek. "The one I'm to wed!"

"Over my dead body!" roared the fearless knight.

"Over your dead body," Shrek agreed.

"Not so brave, thou churlish knave!" countered the knight.

"Do me the honor to step aside, so Shrek can go to meet his bride," Shrek commanded.

"Magician's mercury, plumber's lead, I smite your stupid, scabby head." And the knight smote.

Shrek popped his eyes, opened his trap, and bellowed a blast of fire.
The knight, red-hot, dove into the stagnant moat.

With a nasty snort of triumph, Shrek crossed the bridge and marched
into the castle. And there, for the first time ever, he found out what fear was.

All around him were hundreds of hideous creatures. He was so appalled
he could barely manage to spit a bit of flame. All those horrid others
spat back. He started to run; they all ran. He lashed out at the nearest one,
but what he struck was glass.

Shrek was in the Hall of Mirrors! "They're all me!" he yodeled. "ALL ME!" He faced himself, full of rabid self-esteem, happier than ever to be exactly what he was.

He strode on in and his fat lips fell open. There before him was the most stunningly ugly princess on the surface of the planet.

"Apple Strudel," Shrek sighed.

"Cockadoodoodle," cooed the princess.

Said Shrek: "Your horny warts, your rosy wens,
                        Like slimy bogs and fusty fens,
                        Thrill me."

Said the princess: "Your lumpy nose, your pointy head,
                        Your wicked eyes, so livid red,
                        Just kill me."

Said Shrek: "Oh, ghastly you,   "I could go on,
             With lips of blue,   I know you know
             Your ruddy eyes   The reason why
             With carmine sties   I love you so—
             Enchant me.   You're ugh-ly!"

Said the princess: "Your nose is so hairy,
                  Oh, let us not tarry,
                  Your look is so scary,
                  I think we should marry."

Shrek snapped at her nose. She nipped at his ear. They clawed their way into each other's arms. Like fire and smoke, these two belonged together.

So they got hitched as soon as possible. And they lived horribly ever after, scaring the socks off all who fell afoul of them.